W9-BKU-228

sto

WADDY AND HIS BROTHER

WADDY AND HIS BROTHER

by
PATRICIA COOMBS

Lothrop, Lee & Shepard Co., Inc., New York

©1963 by Patricia Coombs. Library of Congress Catalog Card Number: 63-16783. All rights reserved. Printed in the U.S.A.

Waddy woke up and bounced out of bed. He washed his face. He brushed his teeth. He put on his shirt and trousers and bounced downstairs.

His big sister shouted: "MOTHER! Make Waddy keep quiet!" And his big brother yelled: "MOTHER! Waddy stood on the toothpaste again!"

Waddy went into the kitchen. His mother was feeding the baby.

Waddy sat down at the table. He looked at his bowl of oatmeal. He stuck a paw in. It was cold. He looked at his cup of milk. He stuck a paw in. It was warm.

Waddy looked at the baby. It was all that baby's fault. The baby spoiled everything.

Nobody cared about Waddy any more. All they cared about was that *baby*. No matter what the baby did they smiled. But if Waddy did anything he got scolded.

Waddy picked up his bowl and turned it upside down on top of his head. Milk and sugar and oatmeal dripped slowly over his nose and ears and down his neck.

"UGH! What a mess!" his big sister and his
big brother said. But they didn't really care, and
went off to school.

Waddy peeked out from under the bowl. His
mother was putting the baby in the playpen and
making silly noises for the baby and giving the
baby toys to play with.

Mother Raccoon began to clear the table. She looked at Waddy. "Oh, Waddy! What have you done now!" she cried. "Run upstairs and take a bath. And don't get oatmeal all over the walls."

Waddy climbed slowly up the stairs. He got into the bathtub and turned the water on.

Waddy sat in the bathtub and thought very sad thoughts. Maybe he would go away, someplace where he'd never have to wash, or try to find the cap to the toothpaste, or be scolded. He thought how sorry his family would be, how much they would miss him.

"Waddy! Waddy!" his mother was calling him.

"Waddy! Hurry and get dressed. I need you. It's very important!" called Mother Raccoon.

Waddy sat straight up and listened. "Needs me? Needs ME?" Waddy ducked under the water and then bounced out of the tub.

He bounced into his room and got dressed.

He bounced downstairs. His mother was waiting for him. She looked worried.

"Aunt Ruth just called," said Mother Raccoon. "She is sick in bed with chicken pox. I must go and take her some groceries and medicine, and I can't take you and the baby with me."

Waddy nodded. "We'd catch chicken pox," said Waddy.

"That's right," said Mother Raccoon. She smiled. She was smiling at HIM.

"You are growing up," said Mother Raccoon. "And this is a grown-up job I'd like you to do for me. Do you think you can watch the baby for a little while?"

"Oh, yes, Mother!" shouted Waddy, bouncing up and down. "I'll wash the dishes and make the beds and . . ."

Mother Raccoon patted him on the head. "Just taking care of the baby is a big enough job."

Mother Raccoon put on her bonnet and shawl and got her basket ready. She leaned down and kissed Waddy goodbye.

Waddy stood at the door and waved to his mother. Mother Raccoon looked back, worried. Waddy waved and bounced up and down.

When his mother had gone, Waddy closed the
door. He got out an apron.

It was a great deal too long, but by folding it
up and tucking it under, Waddy got it to stay on.

Waddy looked over at the baby and frowned.
"You be good," said Waddy. "I'll show you what
it's like to be grown up. I'm going to wash the
dishes."

Waddy pulled a stool over to the sink and
sloshed the dishes around in the water.

Waddy stepped down from the stool to get a towel. His feet got tangled up in the apron and he fell on the floor. Waddy wrapped the apron around himself again. But as soon as he took a step he tripped and fell down. When he got his nose out from under the apron he saw the baby watching him. The baby was laughing and bouncing up and down.

"Hey!" said Waddy, "you think I'm funny! I can be lots funnier, just watch!"

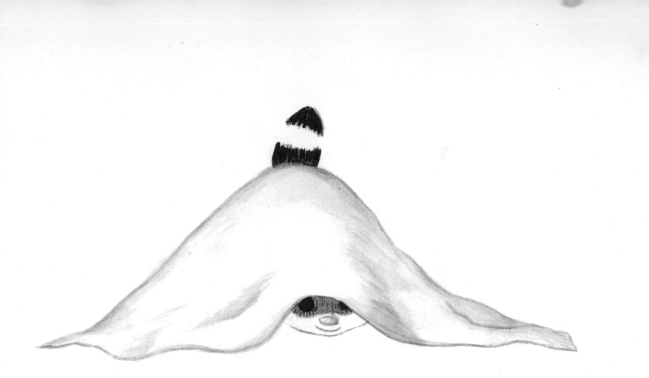

Waddy pulled the apron back over his head and crawled around and around the playpen, growling like a lion. The baby laughed and shouted.

"Here, you try it," said Waddy.

The baby tried crawling with the apron on top of him but it didn't work. He just got all tangled up.

"Never mind, baby," said Waddy. "You're not big enough yet. But you just keep watching me and you'll learn a lot of things."

"Now," said Waddy, "I'll show you how to dry dishes. When you're bigger, maybe next week, I'll let you dry the spoons."

Waddy was drying the oatmeal pan when it dropped. The baby laughed. Waddy dropped the lid. The baby shouted. Waddy grabbed the spoons and forks and dropped them. They made a wonderful clatter and Waddy and the baby laughed and laughed.

"Here," said Waddy, "this is even better." He gave the baby a pan and a spoon. Waddy got a bigger pan for himself and a great big spoon. He put the dish-towel over his head for a hat and marched around and around, banging on the pan.

The baby banged on his pan and shouted and banged and bounced up and down.

"You learned to do that very well," said Waddy. "Now I will show you something else." Waddy climbed up and got a box of crackers. He gave some to the baby.

"You take the crackers and crumble them up,
and throw them all around," said Waddy. "When
there are enough crumbs, I'll show you how to
sweep the floor."

Waddy and the baby crumbled up crackers
and threw them in the air.

Waddy got the broom and started to sweep, but there were so many crumbs the baby began to sneeze. Waddy sneezed.

"I'll show you how to play horse, instead," said Waddy. He hung a towel over the end of the broom and galloped around the kitchen shouting "GIDDYAP!"

"Gup!" shouted the baby. The baby sat on the pan and tried to gallop like Waddy. He fell over and laughed. And Waddy laughed so hard at the baby he rolled over and kicked his feet in the air.

Waddy and the baby had played so hard and laughed so much they were tired. Waddy looked out the window to see if Mother Raccoon was coming back.

"Mother said a little while, and I think it has been a big while. Maybe Aunt Ruth got sicker."

The baby rubbed his eyes and began to cry.

"Poor baby," said Waddy. "I'll get you a pillow."

Waddy put the pillow in the playpen. There was a small hole in one end of the pillow and feathers floated out.

The baby stopped crying. He tried to catch the feathers, and so did Waddy. The baby pulled more feathers out of the pillow and threw them into the air and laughed. Waddy blew at the feathers and they floated way up and then down again.

Waddy waved a towel in the air, and the feathers came down like snow all over everything.

After a while, the baby began to cry again. Waddy looked at the baby.

"I think you are hungry," said Waddy. "I'm hungry too."

Waddy got out the strawberry jam and some bread. He put lots and lots of strawberry jam on the bread and gave a piece to the baby, and Waddy ate his piece.

The baby was licking the jam off the bread. The jam stuck to his nose and his chin and his face and his paws.

Waddy fixed another piece of bread with lots of jam for himself and for the baby. The baby bounced up and down. Every time he bounced more feathers flew up into the air. When the feathers came down they stuck to the jam on the baby's face and paws.

Waddy looked at the baby. "You look like some funny kind of bird," said Waddy. "I'd better get into the playpen with you and get you cleaned up."

But when Waddy tried to get the feathers off the baby, the feathers stuck to Waddy's paws. So Waddy waved his paws like wings and crowed for the baby. And the baby laughed and waved his paws and tried to crow, too.

At last the baby leaned back against the pillow and yawned.

Waddy leaned back against the pillow beside the baby and he yawned.

The baby yawned again and closed his eyes.

Waddy yawned again and closed his eyes. And in a few minutes Waddy and the baby were fast asleep.

Mother Raccoon came hurrying up the path saying "Oh dear, oh dear, oh dear!" She had gotten lost in a blackberry thicket on the way home. Her shawl was torn and she was very worried about Waddy and the baby! She had run until she was out of breath.

Mother Raccoon opened the door. Feathers flew across the floor. She looked at the mess.

"Oh my goodness!" cried Mother Raccoon. Then she saw Waddy and the baby asleep together in the playpen, and she smiled.

Mother Raccoon hung up her bonnet and shawl and started to pick up the pots and pans and lids and spoons. Then Waddy's big brother and big sister came home.

"UGH!" they yelled.

"HAH HAH CHOO!" sneezed big brother.

"OOOF!" cried big sister, stepping in some jam. "MOTHER! What have you been doing?"

Waddy woke up. Mother Raccoon reached down and picked him up in her arms.

"I got lost in the blueberry thicket on the way home from Aunt Ruth's house. And Waddy has taken care of the baby for me all this time. He did a good job."

Mother Raccoon took Waddy upstairs and gave him a bath.

"You know what, Mother?" said Waddy.

"No," said Mother Raccoon, "what?"

"I'm teaching the baby how to do things. And he thinks I'm funny. He thinks I'm about the funniest person in the whole family."

That night, Mother Raccoon told Father Raccoon how she had gotten lost and how Waddy had taken care of the baby for her.

And Father Raccoon said, "Well, well, well," and patted Waddy on the back.

And Waddy told his father how he had showed the baby how to play horse, and bang on kettles, and crow like a rooster.

After supper Waddy sat in his father's chair and read the baby a story before bedtime. The baby tried to chew the book and Waddy showed him how to look at the pictures instead of chewing them.

And everybody smiled at Waddy. Even his big brother and his big sister.